TO
JOSH —
LIFE IS
FULL OF
ADVENTURE!

Blackbear
Pirate

The Search for Captain Ben

The Search for Captain Ben

Written by
Steve Buckley

Illustrated by
Ruth Palmer

More Blackbear the Pirate Adventures:

Blackbear the Pirate
Calico's Ghost
The Treasure Hunt

THE SEARCH FOR CAPTAIN BEN
Copyright © 2014 by Steve Buckley
All rights reserved

(The search for Captain Ben: A Blackbear the Pirate Adventure
Text & illustrations copyright © 2011 by Steve Buckley)

Published by Premiere
307 Orchard City Drive
Suite 210
Campbell, CA 95008 USA
info@fastpencil.com
http://premiere.fastpencil.com

3dMagicAction is a trademark of Courier Corporation

Manufactured in China by Oceanic Graphic International Inc.
33755801 2014

First Edition

Old pirates never die,
they just sail beyond the horizon.

Blackbear the Pirate and his faithful crew were sailing about on his great pirate ship when the first mate, Izzy Paws, called out, "I think we are being followed!"

Blackbear saw that it was Stark the Whale Shark, who appeared to be in a hurry. "Ahoy, Mr. Stark!" hailed Blackbear the Pirate.

"Ahoy, Captain Blackbear," exclaimed Stark, "I'm so glad I found you!"

Stark brought Blackbear and the crew of the Annie some startling news.

"Old Captain Ben is missing," Stark said sadly, "and is feared to be lost at sea!"

"Captain Ben is lost at sea?" questioned Barty, the wisest member of the crew.

"Who is Captain Ben?" asked LeKidd, the youngest mate aboard the Annie.

"Captain Ben was the greatest captain to sail the seven seas!" declared Calico, the saltiest sea bear in the crew.

"To sail the seven seas!" squawked Pawly the Parrot.

"He truly was a great captain," agreed Bonnie, the cook aboard the Annie.

"He still is," insisted Blackbear the Pirate, "and he taught me everything I know."

Blackbear was eager to learn what had happened to his old friend and teacher, so he turned the Annie north towards Bearavaria where Captain Ben lived aboard his ship, the Adventure.

"Aye there, Capt'n, seems like we need a push to help the Annie make way," observed Izzy as the wind died down.

"Perhaps the Annie will have to drift with the waves, unless..." Blackbear paused as he raised his spyglass to look out over the deep blue sea.

Blackbear saw two large white figures swimming towards them. It was Mandy and Molly, the twin white whales and friends of Blackbear. They, too, had heard that Captain Ben was missing, and had come to help.

"Ahoy to you and your crew, Captain Blackbear," the twins sang out, "Can we lend you a fin?"

"We could use a little push until we get the wind back in our sails," admitted Blackbear the Pirate.

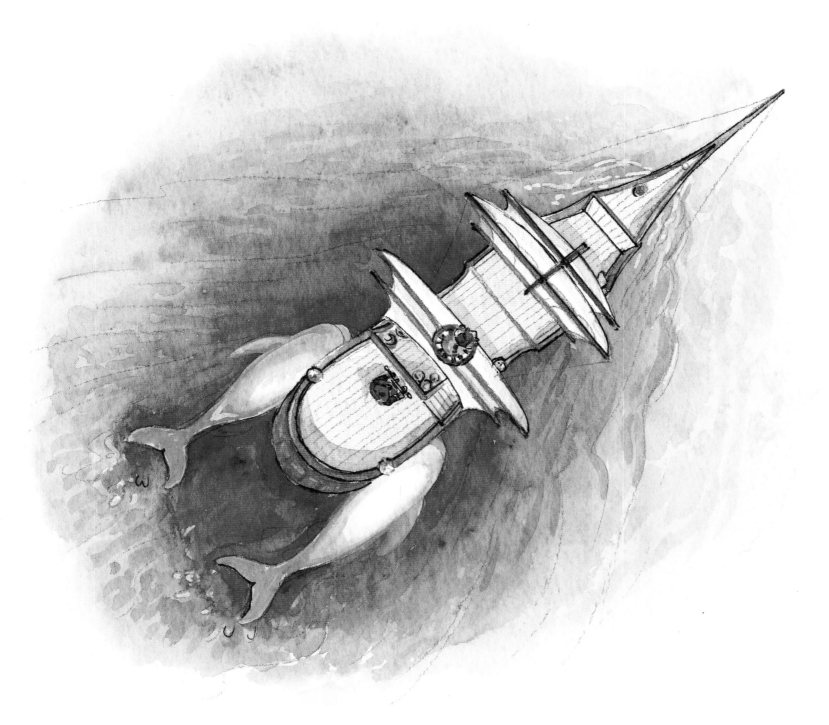

Mandy and Molly leaned against the sides of the Annie, and with the flip of their giant tail fins they splashed the great ship through the water even faster than the wind could carry her.

In no time at all they arrived at the island of Bearavaria, and hastily made their way to the home of Calico's Uncle Avery who also lived on the island. Uncle Avery confirmed the news that Captain Ben was lost at sea.

"Aye there maties, there be no way old Capt'n Ben can be lost at sea," claimed Calico.

"Lost at sea!" squawked Pawly the Parrot.

"Perhaps Captain Ben sailed the Adventure around to the far side of the island," suggested Barty.

"And has run into some sort of trouble there," added LeKidd.

Uncle Avery and all of Bearavaria joined in a search for Captain Ben. They looked all around the island, but there was no sign of him or his ship. They were all very sad at the idea of never seeing Captain Ben again.

"I'm afraid there is nothing more we can do," said Uncle Avery.

"Tis a dark day in the making," whispered Izzy to Blackbear the Pirate.

"Not on my watch!" declared Blackbear, as he turned and stared out at the rolling blue water.

Blackbear the Pirate was a faithful friend and he was not about to give up hope in finding Captain Ben.

Blackbear and his crew went back aboard the Annie and with Mandy and Molly alongside they set off in search of Captain Ben.

"Aye there Capt'n, how do you know which way we should go?" asked Calico.

"We will just follow the flow of the ice!" replied Blackbear.

Blackbear the Pirate was a very smart captain, and he knew where to take the Annie to have the best chance of finding Captain Ben.

Early the next morning LeKidd suddenly cried out from the crow's nest, "I think I see something!"

"It's the top of a ship's mast," moaned Bonnie as the Annie sailed closer.

"Captain Ben's ship must have run into the ice and sunk," realized Barty.

Mandy and Molly quickly swam over to where the mast lay against the iceberg. Going around to the other side, they called out, "The mast isn't the only thing here!"

"Shiver me timbers!" roared Calico when he saw what they had found.

"Shiver me timbers!" squawked Pawly the Parrot as he flew out over the ice.

As the crew looked out over the water, Mandy and Molly swam towards the Annie with Captain Ben standing on their backs.

"Your teacher taught you well," Bonnie said as she smiled proudly at Blackbear.

"It's good to see you old friend!" Blackbear told Captain Ben as he climbed aboard the Annie.

"It's good to be seen," agreed Captain Ben, "But look at what has happened to my ship!"

"Aye there, Capt'n Ben, the Adventure has seen a better day," observed Izzy.

"Is there nothing we can do?" asked LeKidd.

"What's done is done," replied Bonnie, as she handed Captain Ben a bowl of warm stew.

"That may be true," agreed Blackbear the Pirate, "but there are some things that can be undone."

"And we can help undo them!" offered Mandy and Molly.

"And so can I!" shouted Stark the Whale Shark as he swam up to lend a fin.

Blackbear the Pirate was a skillful captain, and he knew exactly what to do. He tossed a large rope around the mast of the Adventure, and gave a nod to Stark and the twins, sending them beneath the waves.

Blackbear turned with the wind, pulling on the Adventure as the others pushed from below. Suddenly, the ship broke free from the ice and sprang to the surface of the sea.

"Hooray, Hooray!" shouted the crew of the Annie.

"How can I ever repay you?" asked a teary eyed Captain Ben, "You saved me and my ship!"

"You already have," assured Blackbear as he gave Captain Ben a big bear hug, "You taught me everything I know!"

Captain Ben went back aboard his ship, and waved good-bye. The wind filled the Annie's sails, and Blackbear the Pirate and his faithful crew headed south to go in search of their next great adventure.